W9-ACU-528

Dear Parent:

Congratulations! Your child is taking the first steps on an exciting journey. The destination? Independent reading!

STEP INTO READING® will help your child get there. The program offers five steps to reading success. Each step includes fun stories and colorful art. There are also Step into Reading Sticker Books, Step into Reading Math Readers, Step into Reading Phonics Readers, Step into Reading Write-In Readers, and Step into Reading Phonics Boxed Sets—a complete literacy program with something for every child.

Learning to Read, Step by Step!

Ready to Read   Preschool–Kindergarten
• big type and easy words • rhyme and rhythm • picture clues
For children who know the alphabet and are eager to begin reading.

Reading with Help   Preschool–Grade 1
• basic vocabulary • short sentences • simple stories
For children who recognize familiar words and sound out new words with help.

Reading on Your Own   Grades 1–3
• engaging characters • easy-to-follow plots • popular topics
For children who are ready to read on their own.

Reading Paragraphs   Grades 2–3
• challenging vocabulary • short paragraphs • exciting stories
For newly independent readers who read simple sentences with confidence.

Ready for Chapters   Grades 2–4
• chapters • longer paragraphs • full-color art
For children who want to take the plunge into chapter books but still like colorful pictures.

STEP INTO READING® is designed to give every child a successful reading experience. The grade levels are only guides. Children can progress through the steps at their own speed, developing confidence in their reading, no matter what their grade.

Remember, a lifetime love of reading starts with a single step!

Visit us on the Web!
StepIntoReading.com
randomhouse.com/kids

Educators and librarians, for a variety of teaching tools, visit us at RHTeachersLibrarians.com

ISBN: 978-0-449-81890-9 (trade) – ISBN: 978-0-449-81891-6 (lib. bdg.)

Printed in the United States of America 10 9 8 7 6 5 4 3 2

nickelodeon TEAM UMIZOOMI™

OUTER-SPACE CHASE

Adapted by John Cabell

Based on the original screenplay by Dustin Ferrer

Illustrated by Jason Fruchter

Random House 🏠 New York

Team Umizoomi visits
the Umi City
Space Center.
DoorMouse takes
their tickets.

Milli, Geo, and Bot see
moon rocks and
a space suit.

They also see
a giant rocket!

DoorMouse opens
his lunch box.
His cheese rolls away!

The cheese rolls
onto the rocket.
DoorMouse
chases it.

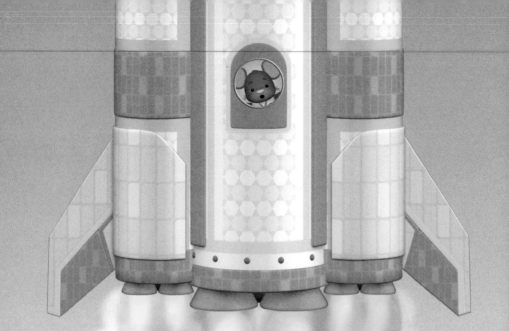

The rocket blasts off!

DoorMouse is on it!

Team Umizoomi must
save DoorMouse.
It's time for action!

Geo makes a rocket!

Super Shapes!

10, 9, 8, 7, 6,

5, 4, 3, 2, 1.

The rocket takes off!

Team Umizoomi
is in space.
Watch out for comets!

A comet hits
the rocket!
The boosters fall off!

Team Umizoomi looks
for the boosters.
Team Umizoomi meets
an alien.

He is wearing
the boosters.
They keep
his feet warm.

Bot gives the
alien some socks.

The alien gives
Bot the boosters.

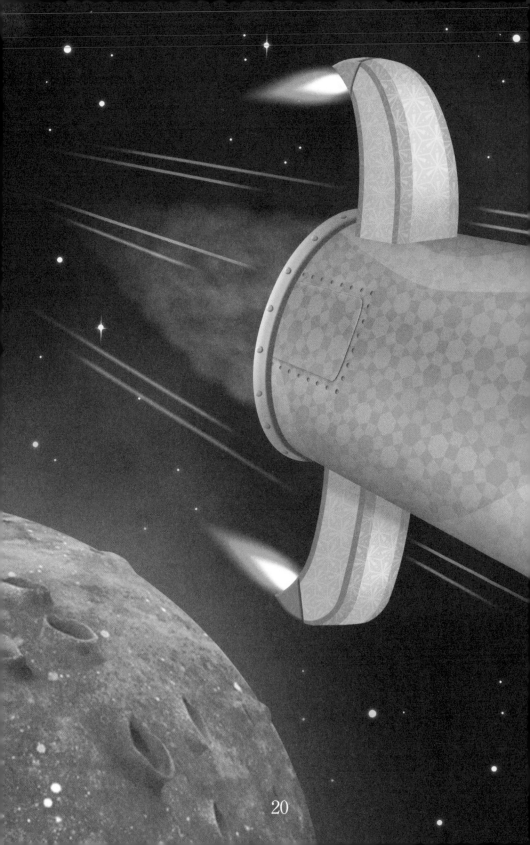

The rocket is fixed!

The team must fly
really fast.
They need to find
a Speedy Star.

Milli will find
the Speedy Star.
Pattern Power!

The pattern is
red, yellow, blue.
Milli finds
the Speedy Star!

Team Umizoomi's rocket
flies through the star.
The rocket goes
really fast!

Team Umizoomi finds
DoorMouse's rocket.
It is going to crash
into Mars!

"We need to catch
DoorMouse's rocket!"
says Bot.

Team Umizoomi's rocket
has a Space Magnet.

The Space Magnet
catches the rocket!

DoorMouse is

back on Earth!

"We saved DoorMouse!"
says Geo.

2, 4, 6, 8!

Everybody Crazy Shake!